A Thousand Splendid Stars

Ariel C. Cabasag

Ukiyoto Publishing

All global publishing rights are held by

Ukiyoto Publishing

Published in 2025

Content Copyright © Ariel C. Cabasag

ISBN 9789370096745

All rights reserved.
No part of this publication may be reproduced, transmitted, or stored in a retrieval system, in any form by any means, electronic, mechanical, photocopying, recording or otherwise, without the prior permission of the publisher.

The moral rights of the author have been asserted.

This is a work of fiction. Names, characters, businesses, places, events, locales, and incidents are either the products of the author's imagination or used in a fictitious manner. Any resemblance to actual persons, living or dead, or actual events is purely coincidental.

This book is sold subject to the condition that it shall not by way of trade or otherwise, be lent, resold, hired out or otherwise circulated, without the publisher's prior consent, in any form of binding or cover other than that in which it is published.

www.ukiyoto.com

A great story can be found above the clouds, where thousands of stars relentlessly appeal to the eyes. There's no such story as impeccable, due to readers' different preferences. However, reading the peculiar stories that can be found above the magnificent stars might have gripped the eyes: to keep on reading the fictional story.

Let us glimpse at the magnificent stars, where appealing tales can be found. Each light of the star guides you, how to dwell with someone whom you really love the most. Let us be upbeat for everything under the sun.

Ariel C. Cabasag, LPT, MATELL
Published author/Poet
English Professor in the Philippines
Manila City, Philippines

Acknowledgment

I deeply appreciate the importance of acceptance. It's my pleasure to let you know how chuffed I am. To be part of this opportunity is an arduous process; however, you have acknowledged my efforts and dreams to shine as a fictional author. I believe that many writers want to be acknowledged for their talents in writing. Fortunately, you have selected and appreciated my wills and arms in transforming the text to reality.

This book contains several stories that sound similar to the essence of a star. Writing serves a pleasure to a writer like me, who wishes to share his/her thoughts or story in the universe. The impact of the story might be negative or affirmative to the readers, which I appreciate the most. However, the author won't know about the reader's impact or impression of this story without the Ukiyoto publishing company. With that, I am very thankful for the acceptance of my book.

I truly understand that my writing style can be perfect to everyone, due to readers' preferences. Despite that, I am hoping that someone will acknowledge and appreciate my fictional story. I didn't write this story, using my pen, I just wrote it using the green leaf, which inspires me to move forward as I glimpsed at the splendid stars in the sky.

Contents

Overview	1
Fiction 1: Star Hauled the Sea	2
Fiction 2: Till I Miss You	5
Fiction 3: Eyeing My Crush	8
Fiction 4: Seeing You Over My Dreams	11
Fiction 5: Holding You Over My Eyes	15
About the Author	18
Thank You Letter	19

Overview

This novel contains five compelling stories, which accentuated the essence of stars in the universe. **The first story narrated about commitment and loyalty to the person whom he really loved the most; indeed, a man made everything just to carry on their love.** *While the second story highlighted a tragedy: a man became a famous king, and he secretly loved someone.* However, *his father's death dwelled over his mind, to dictate over his mind of killing the woman, whom he sincerely loved the most.*

While the **third story narrated about his crush, a woman eventually grips his eyes, hands painted by the snow. The star reflected on their nights till the man decided to sincerely love her.** *The* **fourth story** *emphasized about* **a man who craved to share his intense love, exclusively for her; however, he hunkered to focus his eyes on heaven rather than her.** *While* **the fifth story, it pointed out a tragic-comedy, where a man discovered his gender identity after he found his lover.** *He didn't disclose his feelings to the man, but when the time came, he fell in love with a guy, whom he put his eyes. However, he can't leave his wife, due to their marriage.*

There's no good story without the essence of star in the universe; indeed, the star makes the story to be compelling, which endlessly gripped the readers to attach their eyes book.

Let us find out the essence of stars in the story. How can the word star can be applied to the character's lives?

Fiction 1: Star Hauled the Sea

It's been a million nights of candidly revealing the thunder: she's not happy with him. The thunder armed the star's secret, which changed his life, to make the star happy. And taught to leave her secrets; otherwise, she might be forever a snow.

Intertwined by the electrifying lights beside Kylee, a secret creature by the stars. Her gloom unveiled as a lightning at night; however, she dwelled as a peculiar lady: as the sunrise appeared above the hills. In the village, millions of eyes couldn't behold how she strolled on the land, except Javier who put the secret place about her existence. Javier, on the other hand, is one of Kylee's neighbors, who put his lovely eyes at Kyle's window till sunset. He tarried her shadow over his dreams, yet the night failure of bonking them apart.

Javier painted what the eyes stared at night; Kylee, a beautiful star. It often crossed his mind that the star, deemed as the savior in the universe. His three eyes embellished, as she often cloyed over the mountains. How the man carried her soul and dreams.

Meanwhile, Jariv came to the hills as a powerful thunder in the universe. His eyes drenched down to the glistening lights, till the thunder and star fastened their arms on the hills. Clipping their lights together, Jariv's arms swirled; how the star carried the bees in the mounds.

It's a candied night of rhyming the hills. Sadly, the lightning lessened its lights, due to the intensity of the moon; against the rules of the sun to her. The star might fade in the universe, Kylee mouthed to the moon of living her life again. However, the moon was unable to interpret her language.

Not eyeing her, Jariv tightly gripped the invisible star till the lady came back again. Hence, the moon handed Jariv, which led to her existence. However, Jariv had conditions: to be with him in the tunnel, which might cause the clouds to fall to the sea. Being part of his journey is a blessing, yet she craved to live as human beings, to extend their bond together.

It took a year of thinking till Kylee made up her mind of putting his ears at Jariv's secrets. Believing, this made her life a whale of time; hence, she put her hands at Jariv's eyes which has been creating a thousand lights, till it became a star.

The more the star becomes bigger, the more human beings have faced challenges in their lives like death and poverty. During the day, the painted star displayed its bewitching smiles, which dwelled by wonderful feelings for humankind. Jariv made something special, just to make Kylee happy. That night, he brought her to the Loveth place, where their eyes swirled. Bridging their eyes, it made Kylee feel thrilled, what the guy did to him.

It's been thirty nights of not seeing Kylee over his dreams. Javier slept beside his painting; however, his mind dreamt about Kylee, who handed Jariv's hands till the end of the universe. Instead of feeling down in the dumps, Javier painted a supertree, which looked like Kylee's image. In the town, many people lost their hope to survive: to seeing what Javier portrayed. Each leaf pulled their feet to move forward with their lives.

*The night of seeing the painted tree, Kylee withered her feelings to Jariv. Instead of pretending in front of him, she told him that," **love ends,**." Then, Jariv offered through painting a flower like a mountain. She valued what Jariv did to that night; however, her eyes got attracted to the supertree, which had been painted by Javier. In their situation, Jariv couldn't let his love out for her, however, his light is attached to Kylee's arms. Due to their complicated situation, Jariv tolerated Kylee to depart; however, she's not allowed to marry anyone. Otherwise, she will regret everything, once she thinks it may happen.*

One day, Kylee visited the wonderland where Javier painted the tree. She tirelessly tried of touching the painted leaf, however the leaf fell. That time, she looked like a human being, yet she couldn't recall what she had been dreaming about. That night, she stayed under the leaf which was painted by Javier.

*In the middle of the night, Javier woke up, due to the tears falling down onto his bed. His eyes gazed at the vivid leaf gripped by his arms. As he arrived at the supertree, the leaf gripped him till dawn. Full of astonishment, his eyes brimmed with the painted photo, which was made by Javier." **Is this you?"***

*Then, Javier tolerated her on reading what he wrote for her," **seeing you like an angel till forever. Life seems withered as nothing, once I can't put my pen in you."** Then," **you made me special."** Meanwhile, the supertree fell apart; it thrilled what they did under the leaves. However, Kylee felt* scared because she's already married to Jariv. Over her mind Jariv tells her, "**once you will leave me ultimately, you will regret.**" To be frank, Kylee inveigled him about her situation," we can do it, Kylee."

"**What?** "Kylee asked.

"**We can do it, let me paint a leaf, so he could think that you are there,**" Javier.

"**What if he knows our connection?**" She's doubtful.

Meanwhile, Jariv knocked the hills of their nights via the thunder; however, his ears loudly heard," **let us get out,**" he pulled out the tree using his arms. What he saw himself, who is currently sleeping beside the man. He wanted to relieve his terrible feelings; however, the thunder came out from his lovely eyes, which burnt out the entire tree.

That night, the fire ate the supertree, where Javier died, except Kylee. He felt over the moon upon seeing the thunder's actions; however, Kylee's eyes became blind: she mouthed her regret regarding the terrible event. Seeing her situation, Jariv regretted his actions and told her," **I can't do this to you, if you're loyal in my heart.**"

"**Let us consider it as an accident, but you can't heal my eyes anymore,**" she said. Then, she further told him that her love couldn't be blamed," **I am also a human being that has a heart to love him.**"

Instead of leaving her, " **let me put it into my heart in that situation. One thing I could tell you: no matter what you did. You are always in my heart.**" Then, he put his arms to the woman: "**let me bring you to the hemisphere, where I could find a single light as your eyes.**"

That night, the thunder flew to the sky. His hands often gripped her till he found a single light. He put it at Kylee's eyes till she could see the world. There have been times, Jariv made a kingdom in the sky, where he and Kylee lived each other. The kingdom looked like a mountain where Kylee valued and appreciated Jariv's efforts and love. There have times that Kylee fell down the sea; however, Jariv often extended his time to carry on their love each other.

Fiction 2: Till I Miss You

It's a plaintive night as Raven glimpsed at the bay, where he dwelled with Azu, his ravishing lover. The time is fleeting; as he embellished the triumphant hands, which often lay down by his heart. No time of longing to find his match again, what he often put into his mind: to stay with someone, who doesn't live his life; however, his vivid feelings are forever attached to her. **How will I meet her again?**

It's a countless night of putting his life under the snow; still, he casted back, the moment as they put their feelings apart. Indeed, there have been times of seeing her over his dreams; however, his dream is not an impeccable way of reuniting her, but his magnanimous power.

At Belgium kingdom, king Daryl, his father, pledged him of taking over the palace after his death. His face is full of untoward wrinkles, as he loudly heard from king Daryl. He longed to assassinate the king, since Daryl controlled his heart of love with Azu.

It's been a decade of sacrificing his feelings for the woman he loved. He made up his mind to depart the kingdom, and revealed the power of the king. Telling the hidden secrets, the king was unable to breathe till he died.

Raven took over the power of his king, which could help him: to view his lover again. However, Azu was taken by Jay, a classy man in the town. It's a melancholy feeling of looking the king; he met her alone, and told her:

"I killed the king because of my love for you. Why won't you wait for my love?"

"I am sorry, Raven. I really miss you; however, you're already dead over my dreams."

"What if! Let's put our hearts again, Azu," Raven said.

"Hmm, I feel over the moon to love you again, but someone has been loving me for a trillion years," Azu said.

"Let me love you, like how I sincerely miss you."

That moment, Azu bawled about what she did to Raven; indeed, her heart was about to fall into the sea. She wanted to love him again; indeed, she portrayed Raven by her soul and mind, which she couldn't have removed for a trillion years. However, Azu is already pregnant, which she couldn't deny to Jay, who has been loving her for a thousand years.

Due to pensive moments, Raven hugged his king, and aimed to return to his life again. However, his power seems abysmal, what he should do is to accept the veracity. He buried the king at Belgium kingdom, where he often wished to live with Azu.

There have been nights, Raven saw Jay, who carried Azu using his lovely hands. He felt a green-eyed monster looking at them; using his power, let Jay sleep till dawn. Meanwhile, he told Azu about his regrets and wish to love each other again. He could convince Azu to carry on their love; however, king Daryl's voice came to his ears: kill her, so you could thereafter stay with Azu.

Without hesitation, he killed Azu in front of the kingdom. As Jay woke up, he noticed the bloody image and Azu's dead body; he shouted of what he saw. That time, Raven laughed at what he did; unfortunately, Azu became a snow, which couldn't be held by Raven. He has a lot of regrets for his actions, while Jay really missed Azu, who disappeared over his eyes. She's dead in the universe, but Raven always misses her.

> *Raven wrote a piece to Azu:*
>
> **I wish I could meet her**
>
> **I got tempted by my king to kill her.**
>
> **Life seems meaningless without her.**
>
> **With the splendid stars**
>
> **I wish I could hug her again**
>
> **I often longed to plant my feelings in the garden**
>
> **here love often be**
>
> **It's too late to regret**
>
> **But it's not too late to carry on her love**
>
> **Till I miss you**
>
> **Hill seem invisible in the window**
>
> **As snow, I often miss you.**

Jay moved forward with his life after 20 years, while Raven forever regretted what he did to Azu. His life seems fantastic in the universe, but his heart stood like a fire. He badly needs Azu's image, to come back to the universe, what he often feels: to miss her over the sea.

Fiction 3: Eyeing My Crush

Night is like a snow, wherever the eyes gazed at; everything seems as an enticing eyes. Often wondered why the snow kept on gripping the nights. Due to hankered moments, Nicole trudged above the hills, where she found clouds, often grip at her. The moment she moved forward her feet; the more she casted back Cydric, a handsome guy, whom he got infatuated with the most.

It's been high school years until college years, she has been waiting for his perfect time. There have been times, she crossed her way with him; however, Cydric was already taken by someone else. It's a pensive moment to whim; how she faced the disgruntled moments. Despite that, she often wished to meet him in life before leaving the city. Let's accept that all night, she often slipped back, how Cydric secretly changed her life. Will I let him know what I really feel for him? It's been trillion times; however, she may be doubtful.

There was time, Nicole dropped her anonymous letter beside Cydric's car, since they studied in the same University. She always made sure that the guy could read her message. She just let him," **I don't appreciate any arts in the universe, seeing you, I often painted you over my eyes. Letting you know how much I wish to bond and know you more. One thing I could say, you're more than a star, which I often longed to stay with."** Then, *she left the car, what she often thought; the man might read or not.*

Meanwhile, Cydric stayed inside the car; he was curious about the girl outside his car. He craved to get out of his car; however, he felt pensive to see what the girl did. Before leaving the campus, he got out of his car to get it. He finally eyed the letter.

One day, Cydric crossed his way with her; he returned the letter, filled with a lovely smile, which carried Nicole's heart to heaven. He just crossed his eyes at her, which seemed like snow. That moment, Therese, a beautiful woman came and let the guy know; **"let us go to the star bucks."** *Nicole felt ashamed in fore of them; hence, she slowly walked away.*

Due to false hope of waiting for him to be; Nicole made up her mind to depart the city. She altered her life, and buried her bad expectations to the guy, who didn't love her back. What she often thought; the man was already taken.

It's been a year of forgetting the man; she met Ivan, a caring man, who often stayed by her side. He put Nicole's day, like an angel in the sky. With that, Nicole became his friend; however, Ivan wanted to tell his secrets to him. The words are unspoken, but Nicole already knew it. She let him know," *I am not here to look for it: I am here to forget my past."* Then, Ivan smiled at her; he pretended that everything seemed fine, even if it's not.

Despite that, Ivan didn't leave her: he often showed his good character and sassy personality. Seeing such things, Nicole really liked how Ivan cared for her. One night, Ivan drove his car, along with Nicole. Meanwhile, they were talking about their past, which made their nights electrifying. Unexpectedly, the lovely weather turned into snow, where everyone couldn't move, due to the ice, which attached the way, including the car. *"Just stay cool, we can do it."* While Nicole loudly cried.

Similarly, Cydric had difficulty moving forward, due to the snow. He came out from his car; his eyes eyed the stunning girl, who bawled; he put his eyes to the hills, where Nicole stood like a shining star. Can't deny, he felt a green-eyed monster staring at them; indeed, he faced the mirror, what he did to her. As he walked away to aid her; however, the snow dissolved.

At that time, Ivan felt over the moon, as they could move forward to the whimsical way. While Cydric walked as a dead moon in the sky; he missed Nicole very much, like how he loved the unforgettable past.

Now on, Ivan happily dwelled with Nicole as friends, a man who altered Nicole's life to move forward. While Cydric regretted why he ignored the girl, who really valued his presence. Everyday, she wished to live a happy life; he read Nicole's letter, which made him really missed her.

After a year, Ivan made up his mind to leave the city: to focus on his work, however he often promised to carry on their friendship. At the back of the mountain, Nicole really missed him; indeed, she wished to stay with him all over her life.

Due to hopeless moments; Nicole went to the bay, where to contemplate her past. It's been a night of staying at the bay; she casted back, how electrifying she was with someone else. Till, she slept in the wet bay; unexpectedly, the snow came back to the city. She had a difficulty to move forward her way; otherwise, the waves might pull her to the middle ocean. She had a plaintive feeling, while falling to her tears.

It's been a year of working as pilot in the aircraft: Cydric is still wishing to meet Nicole again; indeed, he saw her over his eyes. That time, the aircraft passed above the bay, where Nicole was being pulled by the sea, due to the snow. She loudly heard**," I can't do it without you**." Then, Cydric appeared with his eyes on the window, what he eyed: Nicole's body filled with snow. Without hesitation, Cydric dived into the sea: to save her. Meanwhile, the airplane's door opened, a soft voice came in," ***Nicole, hold my hands***," while Cydric's eyes had triumphant eyes staring at the prepossessing lady. His eyes painted at Nicole's hands, which carried Nicole to enter the airplane.

Feelings can't be measured, what she really felt; the moment her only crush saved her. Inside the plane, Cydric made a compelling tale, in which Nicole discovered that Cydric had been waiting for her to come.

To end-

"With you, I longed to alter the snow" (Cydric)

"I dwell like a snow, but you still saved me, Cydric" (Nicole)

"One thing I could describe you: you look like a shining star, which I often longed to stay with" (Cydric)

Finally, Nicole has already met her dreams: to stay with him. She lived her life in a simple way, but she often felt tickled pink, as Cydric handed her arms till sunset. Cydric made Nicole's life into a sky, where he often passed both day and night. Every time he drove the plane, he painted Nicole's eyes, which often dwelled by his heart.

Fiction 4: Seeing You Over My Dreams

It's been a thousand days of being friends, the moment they met to each other. Couldn't deny, Jewel secretly infatuates the man more than herself. With him, she's satisfied with her life, except for thinking of the man to be part of her dreams, what she has been looking for. However, Juris flawlessly treated her as his friend, due to passion of serving people, as a seminarian; to enlighten the people about how to live life meaningfully in the universe.

It took a million nights of dreaming to be part of his life. Despite their opposite dreams in life, she craved to stay happy at all times with him. In her philosophy, being part of his memory is one of the best dreams that she wanted to have in life.

There was a perfect night as they met on the island, where they put their dreams in life. However, a thousand waves pulled the island, which took a year of staying beside the island, still they were able to survive. Their family thought that they were gone, since it took a million tears of shedding on the window. However, Juris believed that it was the king of heaven who saved them. Instead of recognizing Jewel's feelings, he changed his mind to serve God who will save his soul in down the road. He promised himself to come back and love her back, once he will not be successful as a seminarian in the holy seminary. Knowing by his response, Jewel made her life miserable: indeed, she didn't want to value her life, which took it useless.

There was a night when her wallet fell down on the pathway. It's been a year of looking for her things, till the man called her name, as she trudged in the hotel.

That man seemed classy, the way he looked at her.

Mark (smile): Hello miss, is this you? (while holding the photo)

Jewel (astonished): Yes Sir, where did you get that?

Mark (silent): (his eyes looked at the sun)

Jewel(whispered): Sir, are you still talking to me?

Mark (smile): Ahm, I just found it on the aisle.

Jewel (smile): Thank you.

He met Mark, a man who returned his wallet where Mark found Jewel's photos, and got attracted to it. They became friends till she appreciated how kind he was for her. However, she was more than happy to meet Juris again. It took a year of seeing Mark's efforts till she let him of living her heart.

Couldn't describe how wonderful her life was with him. Everything seemed shining due to his efforts, which make Jewel to stay happy. Hence, she valued everything that the man gave to her. Unfortunately, Juris came back to the city, to meet her as his friend. She did not let him know that she had a boyfriend.

Looking at them, Mark felt uncomfortable till he knew that Jewel enticed Juris the most. Despite that, he wanted Jewel to be happy, despite the hurtache that she felt. One night, Jewel personally told Mark that she had a new boyfriend. What he had expected, Jewel came back just to love him.

It made Mark insane of hearing her words, she had a plan to make her life beautiful. However, Jewel would no longer look at his efforts anymore. He left the world of Goddess but he could not forget Jewel who hurt him the most.

After a few nights, Juris told her that he came back: to say goodbye, since he's now officially a priest. He asked for an apology to her, however Jewel blamed him for everything, like her life seemed meaningless because of him. Unfortunately, Juris wanted to prove his beliefs nor to prove his unconditional love for her.

Meanwhile, to stay alone Jewel's life, she often saw Mark's shadow, which carried her, the time she felt sad. One night, she glanced at Mark in the Cinema who dated with Quinn, his new babe. At the same time, Mark slightly eyed on Jewel's eyes which made him get attracted to her again; however, Jewel's action removed his feelings of loving her again.

Knowing the fact that Jewel was single, Mark met her in the bay to let her know how much he loved her. That time, she personally told him how much she loved him. However, her love was still attached to the priest. What she could do is to wait for him, even if he won't be back to her life again.

On the other hand, Juris had faced many trials in life, as she left his friend. Like he got accident which took a decade to get well; however, he proved his dreams of shaping the people, and let them understand the meaningful life. Being a priest is like an island, but he proved himself to value, what the king of heaven has been giving for him.

One night, Juris dreamt about Jewel's shadow which has helped him to ride the kingdom of heaven, including the woman's voice,**" a better night to speak with you."** As he woke up, he found a shadow beside him.

There have been times, Jewel crossed her way with him on the bridge. Juris told him his dreams which made Jewel cry.

Juris: (cry) I am so sorry Jewel.

Jewel: (silent)

Juris:(cry): Please look at my situation.

Jewel (deep inhale): If I could change the world, I will.

That night, Juris revealed how much he loved her; however, his vision is part of his dreams. Deeply seeing his words, Jewel understood his situation, however she couldn't deny that her dream couldn't be deleted till they might be soul.

After two decades of being a priest, he came back to the city. He visited Jewel's house, however he found an alien who looked at him. Everything has been changed, however his eyes could view her as his friend. He gripped the alien's hands, yet he never felt her heart anymore. Due to Juris's interest in why, Jewel has changed into an alien. He resigned as a priest, and look forward of meeting the lovely star by his eyes.

Will Juris and Jewel prove their dreams?

It took a thousand years of searching for her; it came the time, Juris finally met Jewel under the shining star. He let her know, **"I am back to love you,"** showing his smile at her. While Jewel won't really believed what she eyed in front of her. She moved backward from him;

however, a thousand of wind keep on gripping her tightly. Had a charming voice," **I am back to stay with you till the end, Jewel,"** still Jewel didn't believe him. What she always put to her mind: a priest is still serving at the heart of God. Because of her hesitation, a shining star held at her hands, including the swirled wind; then, an enticing eyes dwelled by her sight. *"Is this you, Jewel?"* Then, Juris smiled," *as I told you trillion times, I am back to loving you more,"* he said.

"It's still unbelievable of hearing your words, but my heart has been painting by your sight," Jewel said.

"Yes, I am unbelievable, yet my feelings looks unmeasurable for you," Juris said.

Then, Jewel smiled as she loudly heard his words, which often painted by her side. Due to the shining star, Jewel and Juris converted their feelings into a green leaf, which often young, like how it inspired people to stay positive: to find for their impeccable happiness. Now on, Jewel and Juris loved painted at the trillion of eyes in the universe, which served as an indelible journey and worthwhile feelings, which often like a green leaf.

Fiction 5: Holding You Over My Eyes

It's been a decade of being friends with Aika, who seems elegant and inspiring to him. There have been times, Earl spent his time with her, when Aika stayed in the hospital, due to the accident. One of the best moments, when Earl feels something sweet and love, the moment he has been staying with her. Aika had a terrible experience with her family, who abandoned her two decades ago. Her traumatic experience had added, as she had experienced such an accident in the village; she didn't expect something good may happen, except to give up her life. However, the more Earl has been countlessly staying with her, she changed her heart into sweet and optimistic for something, which may have happened to her.

A man has proved his triumphant hearts, as good as it is. It took a year when Aika didn't work in the company, due to the complicated situations. Still, Earl did something extraordinary, just to save her life, Venna, his colleague, discouraged him from staying with her. She often thought that Aika is not a perfect match for him. What she wanted to happen, Earl may cross her way, due to her hidden feelings for him. She didn't know that Aika and Earl were friends.

Due to the rumors, Earl shared his heart with Aika. It was accepted by her with faith and unconditional love because of what Earl did to her. She has been loving the man, who tirelessly stayed by her side both night and day.

That night, Venna invited Earl to attend her night in the hotel, due to the special occasion. One of Venna's intentions, to make their nights memorable as friends. As Earl entered the hotel where he drank, along with Venna. That night, Venna had a cousin who seemed so ravishing by Earl's eyes. Indeed, he craved to get to know him, and let him know what he really feels for him. It took five hours for Earl to go to the hotel. In fact, Earl went to another room, where he wore a lady gown. He didn't Venna get enticed at him tonight; she went back to the occasion, where Venna got shocked by what she saw. Instead of flirting with him, she fell down her heart, as she stared at him.

One day, Venna met Aika just to reveal the truth. She convinced Aika to depart from him, due to Earl's gender identity. Seeing what Venna took a photo, which made her got discouraged by what she eyed.

It was a perfect night, Earl crossed his way with Aika; he let her know to leave his life, due to his gender identity. He's a gay, but he couldn't erase their memorable moments. And he strongly let him know that he can be a guy, just to carry on their love till the end.

Will he change his gender identity just for her?

Due to their sweetest dreams in life; Aika happily accepted him. Due to Earl's criticism, he decided to leave his job and start her new life with her. They came to a country, where everyone is accepted to live without criticism. After a year, Earl married Aika and lived happily; however, the guy couldn't produce a child for him. Despite that, Aika showed her unconditional love for him. Indeed, she had shown her commitment and faith to the man, whom she trusted the most.

Will the man pay her love?

One night, Earl decided to search for his job in the town, as promised, he wanted Aika to see his efforts for her. After a week, he started his job in the hotel as a manager, where he met the guy, as his workmate, whom he enticed before. Due to a guy, who put his feelings into the sea, where they secretly put their secrets. In short, Earl has found a man who urged him to show his true color. He didn't want Aika to feel sad; however, he couldn't control himself.

There have been times that Aika has observed something new from him. Most of the time, Earl didn't have enough time for her; however, Earl always let her know," **I always put my eyes on you,"** which can be believable.

In the workplace, Earl often put his eyes to Eric, whom he always put his eyes on. They have been making their nights sweet and wonderful; however, this is the last night of putting up their eyes, since Eric needed to face his new family, which he hid it to Earl. It can be sweet to stay with each other; however, time can't put their hearts together.

It's been ten nights, Earl hasn't met the guy in the workplace. He really felt lonely to stay alone, till he fell down in his tears. Such time, Aika saw him, who lay down in the floor. She just perceived that the man had problems; she hugged him tightly. Then, Earl cried loudly," I am sorry for hurting you."

"What did you do?" Aika asked.

"What I did to you?" Aika asked.

"You can leave me anytime. I lost my secret happiness," he said.

That time, Aika understood what he meant; then, she hugged him tightly. "I can still carry you, Earl."

"You can leave me, Aika. But always remember, I often put my eyes on you, despite my gender identity," he said.

"Why won't you delete it from your mind?"

"You can leave me, I do not deserve to be loved by such a woman," he said.

Despite of what he requested of his wife; Aika didn't leave him. She carried the man to the place where they lived happily; each of them put their eyes together until the end. It takes a decade of putting their eyes together, which really changed Earl's feelings. Now on, he teaches his heart to love Aika rather than to find the man, who had already left him before.

Ends.

About the Author

Ariel C. Cabasag, LPT, MATELL

Ariel has been working as an English instructor and creative writer for almost six years in the Philippines. He's a man who loves letters and language, which really helps me to transform his imagination through creative writing. To him, life is meaningful and worthwhile, as he has expressed himself through writing such masterpieces in English literature.

In addition to that, he's famous instructor in teaching English communication, which further drives him to showcase his talents in poetry and essay writing. Most of his students was really inspired by his talents; indeed, he has received many appreciation letters in teaching.

With regards to his educational background, he took MA in Teaching English Language and Literature at Ateneo University, where he further learned the language. And got idolized some effective professors, who indeed motivated him to love teaching English language. After a year, he became a professor at Far Eastern University, where he published many poems: green letters in the cave and while in the milky way. Meanwhile, he started his second MA in Literary and Cultural Studies at Ateneo de Manila, where he further enhanced his talents in writing: to become globally competitive both writing career and teaching.

Thank You Letter

Dear lovely readers:

    I would like to extend my gratitude for selecting and reading my book in your list. Engaging the text is one of the pleasure ways to dwell our hearts and minds of what we are reading. There might be times that reading seems boring; however, interacting the text may lead to better understanding or build a better connection to the text. I appreciate the moment and time that you have shared with me. I wish you really enjoyed reading my fictional story. Your impression serves as my inspiration in life.

Yours truly,

Ariel